3

STONE ARCH BOOKS
a capstone imprint

STONE ARCH BOOKS™

Published in 2012
A Capstone Imprint
1710 Roe Crest Drive
North Mankato, MN 56003
www.capstonepub.com

Originally published by DC Comics in the U.S. in single magazine form as Young Justice #3.

DC Comics
1700 Broadway, New York, NY 10019
A Warner Bros. Entertainment Company

Printed in the United States of America
in Brainerd, Minnesota.
032012 006672BANGF12

Cataloging-in-Publication Data is available at the Library of Congress website:
ISBN: 978-1-4342-4555-7 (library binding)

Summary: In this action-packed story, a woman is targeted by a covert group of assassins! It's Robin, Kid Flash, and Aqualad to the rescue, but can they save her from the combined menace of Hook and Black Spider?

STONE ARCH BOOKS

Ashley C. Andersen Zantop *Publisher*
Michael Dahl *Editorial Director*
Donald Lemke & Sean Tulien *Editors*
Heather Kindseth *Creative Director*
Brann Garvey *Designer*
Kathy McColley *Production Specialist*

DC COMICS

Scott Peterson & Jim Chadwick *Original U.S. Editors*
Michael McCalister *U.S. Assistant Editor*
Mike Norton *Cover Artist*

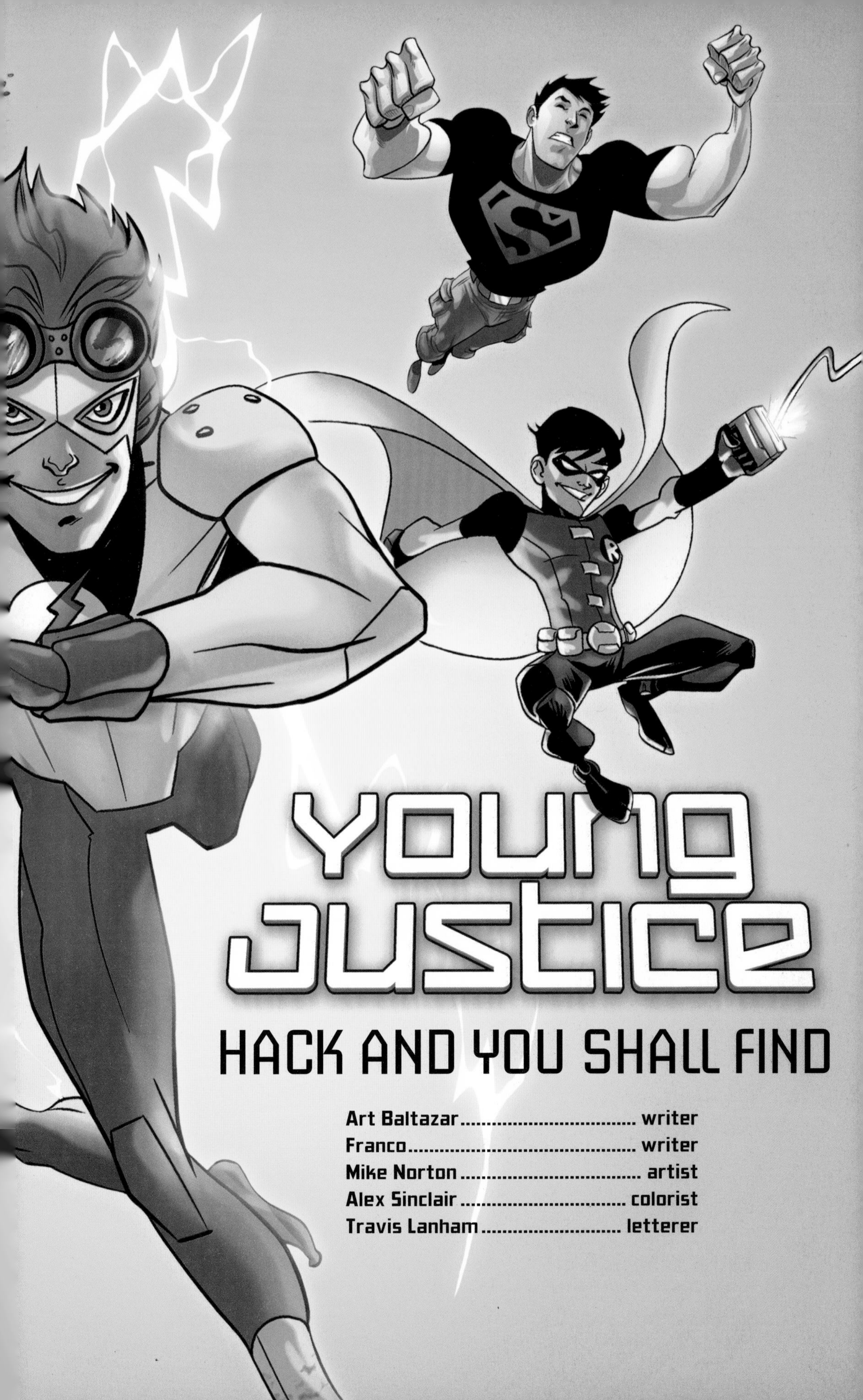

YOUNG JUSTICE

HACK AND YOU SHALL FIND

Art Baltazar.................................... writer
Franco.. writer
Mike Norton .... artist
Alex Sinclair .... colorist
Travis Lanham .... letterer

AQUALAD

AGE: 16 SECRET IDENTITY: Kaldur' Ahm

BIO: Aquaman's apprentice; a cool, calm warrior and leader; totally amphibious with the ability to bend and shape water.

SUPERBOY

AGE: 16 SECRET IDENTITY: Conner Kent

BIO: Cloned from Superman; a shy and uncertain teenager; gifted with super-strength, infrared vision, and leaping abilities

ARTEMIS

AGE: 15 SECRET IDENTITY: Classified

BIO: Green Arrow's niece; a dedicated and tough fighter; extremely talented in both archery and martial arts.

KID FLASH

AGE: 15 SECRET IDENTITY: Wally West

BIO: Partner of the Flash; a competitive team member, often lacking self-control; gifted with super-speed.

ROBIN

AGE: 13 SECRET IDENTITY: Dick Grayson

BIO: Partner of Batman; the youngest member of the team; talented acrobat, martial artist, and hacker.

MISS MARTIAN

AGE: 16 SECRET IDENTITY: M'gann M'orzz

BIO: Martian Manhunter's niece; polite and sweet; ability to shape-shift, read minds, transform, and fly.

THE STORY SO FAR...

While exploring their new headquarters, Superboy and Miss Martian discover an intruder. With help from the Justice League, they're able to subdue the G-gnome from Cadmus, Lex Luthor's research facility. Meanwhile, the other Young Justice members find trouble of their own...

INFINITY ISLAND
JULY 8, 22:14 EDT
OUR EMPLOYERS ARE...ENDING...THEIR RELATIONSHIPS WITH CERTAIN CORPORATIONS THEY WERE PREVIOUSLY DOING BUSINESS WITH.
CUTTING TIES, SO TO SPEAK, BECAUSE OF THE... FIASCO WITH *CADMUS*.
THEY ARE BEING CAUTIOUS. THEY DO NOT WANT ANYTHING TRACED BACK TO THEM.
THIS IS THE REASON WE ARE CALLED INTO ACTION.
WE ARE THE SOLUTION TO THE PROBLEM.
WE ARE THE *LEAGUE OF SHADOWS*.
DO NOT FAIL ME!

SO WHY AM I LOOKING AT A PICTURE OF...?
CENTRAL CITY JULY 9, 13:28 CDT
Cafe Sugar
HER NAME IS GONZALEZ. SELENA GONZALEZ.
AND WE CARE WHY? OTHER THAN THE FACT THAT SHE'S A HOTTIE?
SHE'S HERE IN CENTRAL CITY AND BEING TARGETED FOR A HIT. THERE'S A REASON...
I JUST DON'T KNOW WHAT IT IS YET, BUT I THINK I FOUND SOMETHING THAT MIGHT BE RELATED TO HER.
RELATED HOW?
LOOKING THROUGH SOME OF BATMAN'S FILES I FOUND THAT THERE HAVE BEEN A FEW TARGETS. SEEMINGLY UNRELATED, BUT I'VE CROSS-REFERENCED TONS OF DATA AND I THINK I FOUND A PATTERN.
LOOKING THROUGH? YOU MEAN YOU HACKED INTO BATMAN'S FILES.

ANYWAY...

I THINK THIS CEO MIGHT BE NEXT. ALL OF THE OTHER 'HITS' HAVE BEEN MADE TO LOOK LIKE ACCIDENTS, RANDOM MUGGINGS GONE WRONG, THINGS LIKE THAT--

ANYWAY, I FIGURED WE COULD LOOK INTO THIS.

AND WHAT BROUGHT THIS TO YOUR ATTENTION IN THE FIRST PLACE?

I'VE BEEN LOOKING INTO CADMUS THE LAST COUPLE OF DAYS--CORPORATE HOLDINGS, WHO THEY DO BUSINESS WITH AND SUCH. I NOTICED A FEW PEOPLE THEY'VE DONE BUSINESS WITH SEEM TO MEET WITH UN-TIMELY ACCIDENTS.

YOU WANT US TO LOOK INTO THIS ON A *HUNCH* THAT SOMEONE *MIGHT* HAVE PUT OUT A HIT ON THE CEO OF THIS COMPANY?

COOL!

WHAT ABOUT SUPERBOY AND MISS MARTIAN?

WE DON'T WANT TO GET THEM IN TROUBLE BEFORE THE *TEAM* EVEN GETS GOING, DO WE?
BESIDES, IF YOU THINK ABOUT IT, *WE* HAVEN'T EVEN HAD A REAL OUTING AS A TEAM YET.

LET'S DO IT! C'MON AQUALAD, THIS COULD BE FUN.
OKAY, THINK OF IT AS A TRAINING SESSION, THEN. WE HAVEN'T EVEN HAD ONE OF THOSE AS A TEAM YET.

THEN WHY ARE SUPERBOY AND MISS MARTIAN NOT HERE? THEY ARE PART OF THE TEAM, ARE THEY NOT?
YEAH, BUT... **WE'VE** BEEN AROUND LONGER THAN THEY HAVE AND **WE** HAVEN'T EVEN HAD MUCH INTERACTION WITH EACH OTHER. WE'RE ALWAYS DOING OUR OWN CRIME-FIGHTING THING WITH OUR OWN PARTNERS...
...I FIGURED IT WOULD BE A CHANCE FOR US TO KIND OF CLEAR THE COBWEBS BEFORE WE GET INTO FULL TEAM MODE.

COBWEBS? YOU'VE BEEN HANGING OUT IN DARK CAVES WAY TOO MUCH.
I AM NOT SURE ABOUT THIS...
I AM! COUNT ME IN. YOU THINK SELENA LIKES YOUNGER GUYS?

HOW DO WE KNOW ALL OF THESE RANDOM ACCIDENTS AND MUGGINGS ARE HITS PUT OUT ON PEOPLE AND WHY DO YOU THINK THEY ARE ALL ***RELATED?***
WHO DO YOU THINK IS ***BEHIND*** ALL THIS?
BEHIND IT? HARD TO TELL. COULD BE CADMUS BUT NONE OF THE EVIDENCE POINTS TO THEM. BUT WHO DO I ***THINK*** WAS HIRED TO DO THE JOB ON SELENA GONZALEZ? ***THE LEAGUE OF SHADOWS.***
WHOA! REALLY?
YEAH, I THINK THESE 'ACCIDENTS' WERE EXECUTED BY THEM.
EXECUTED? THAT SEEMS LIKE AN APPROPRIATE WORD.
WAIT. WHO IS THE 'LEAGUE OF SHADOWS'?

WHAT? YOU'VE NEVER HEARD OF THE LEAGUE OF SHADOWS? HAVE YOU BEEN LIVING IN A CAVE OR SOMETHING?
MORE LIKE UNDERWATER.
OH, YEAH...
ALLEGEDLY. NOTHING EVER SEEMS TO GET PROVEN AGAINST THOSE GUYS.
THE LEAGUE OF SHADOWS IS A DEADLY ORGANIZATION WITH THEIR DIRTY HANDS STUCK IN A WHOLE BUNCH OF STUFF ALL OVER THE WORLD. KILLING IS ONLY PART OF THEIR BUSINESS.
SO JUST TO REITERATE... YOU WANT THE THREE OF US TO LOOK INTO WHAT MAY OR MAY NOT BE A SANCTIONED ASSASSINATION ATTEMPT ON THIS CEO, CARRIED OUT BY A COVERT ORGANIZATION CALLED THE LEAGUE OF SHADOWS, WITHOUT ANY OF OUR TEAMMATES...
...AND WITHOUT AUTHORIZATION FROM BATMAN OR THE REST OF THE JUSTICE LEAGUE?
YEAH, PRETTY MUCH.
WHAT ARE WE WAITING FOR?

CENTRAL CITY
JULY 9, 19:54 CDT
WHY IS SHE STILL AT WORK? EVERYONE ELSE WENT HOME HOURS AGO.
COULD YOU NOT CHEW SO LOUD?
AT THIS POINT I WISH HE COULD FEED WITH A FILTER SYSTEM MUCH LIKE A HUMPBACK WHALE WOULD. IT WOULD NOT BE AS NAUSEATING TO WATCH.
HA HA! *GULP!* VERY FUNNY.
COULD YOU JUST KEEP IT DOWN?
CHIPS
WHICH ONE? MY VOICE OR MY CHEWING?
BOTH!
I CAN'T HELP IT. I'M BORED. AND I NEED TO EAT! WE'VE BEEN SITTING HERE FOR HOURS, DO YOU KNOW HOW HARD THAT IS FOR ME TO DO?
SHE'S BEEN IN THAT BUILDING ALL DAY. ALL OF THE EMPLOYEES HAVE GONE HOME, SHE'S ALL ALONE. IF THEY WERE GOING AFTER HER, DON'T YOU THINK THEY WOULD HAVE DONE IT BY NOW?

NO.
HOW DO YOU KNOW THAT, EINSTEIN?
BECAUSE THEY'RE DOING IT RIGHT NOW.
I DON'T SEE ANYTHING--
THERE. BELOW THE WINDOW... MOVEMENT.

WE--
FWOOOOSH
ROBIN, WE--
HAHA HAHAHAHA HAHA
--SHOULD...
≈SIGH≈
THIS IS NOT TEAM BUILDING.
I WOULDN'T WORRY ABOUT *THEM*.

IN A FEW MINUTES, YOU WON'T HAVE A TEAM TO WORRY ABOUT.

HAI!!!

DOESN'T MATTER ONE WAY OR THE OTHER--

BECAUSE YOU--

SLAM
--WON'T BE ABLE TO DO--
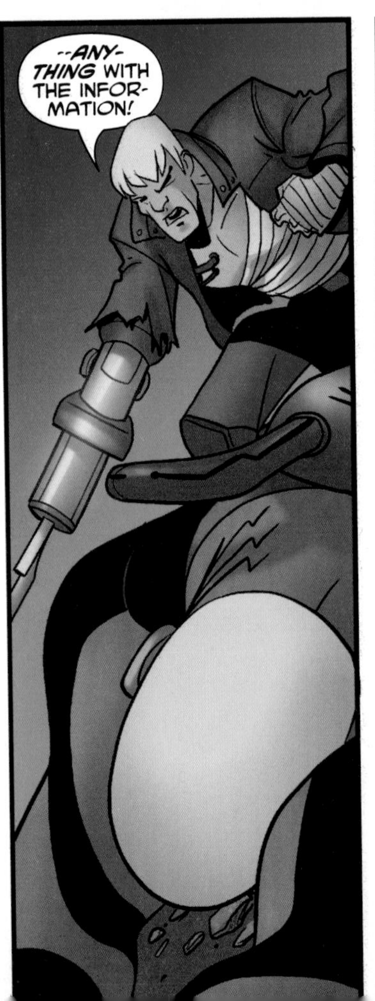
--*ANYTHING* WITH THE INFORMATION!

NOW...

...WHAT SAY WE GO FIND YOUR FRIENDS?

HEY!
'NINJA DUDE'--
FWOOSH
WHOA!
NAME'S
BLACK SPIDER--
'FAST DUDE.'

CRUNCH
AND YOU NEED TO BE FASTER THAN THAT.
MISSED.
DID I?
OOOFF!
LOOK OUT BELOW!

PAF
WOW! WE SO DIDN'T TAKE THAT GUY DOWN!
NO. JUST THE OPPOSITE. HE TOOK US DOWN.
AND HOOK IS THE ONE THAT'S GONNA TAKE YOU OUT!
SAY GOODBYE.
WHAT THE--?

SLAAAAM
DUDE! THIS IS GETTING OUT OF HAND!
WE'RE GONNA TAKE THIS CLOWN DOWN TOGETH--
YOU NEED TO GET UPSTAIRS AND GET TO THE TARGET BEFORE THAT OTHER GUY DOES.
WHAT ABOUT AQUAL--
GO! NOW!

LOOKS LIKE IT'S JUST YOU AND ME, LITTLE BIRD BOY.
I DON'T THINK SO.
BOOF
BOOF
BOOF
WE'LL SEE ABOUT--
--THAT?!
HEY, JUST IN TIME! BY THE WAY, ARE YOU BUSY FRIDAY NIGHT?

THWAP
THWAP
THWAP
C'MON, LADY! WE'VE GOT TO GET OUT OF HERE!

SORRY FOR THE DASH AND GRAB, LADY, BUT I GOTTA GET BACK TO MY--

--FRIENDS?
EXIT

LOOKS LIKE YOUR FRIENDS LEFT YOU HIGH AND DRY!

HEY! CAPTAIN HOOK!
UGH!

GOTTA HELP MY BUDDY! BE RIGHT BACK! YOU STAY *RIGHT HERE!*
KID FLASH! MANEUVER 63!
ROBIN! HIGH AND LOW!
OOOOFF!
UGH!
WHAT WERE YOU DOING?
ME? I SAID HIGH AND LOW! WHEN FLASH AND I TACKLE A BADDIE--
I'M *NOT* THE FLASH!
NO DUH! WHERE'S AQUAL--?
THE GUY JUST GOT SHOT THROUGH A WALL! HE'S GONNA BE OUT FOR A WHILE!
THUD

SERIOUSLY? AGAIN?
FWISSH

KID FLASH!

WHUD
UUUUFF!

ROBIN!

UH-OH.

WE NEED TO GET OUT OF THIS.
AQUALAD IS STILL OUT, I THINK...
WHAT? ...WHERE AM I?
YOU'RE AWAKE? GOOD, BUT WE HAVE SOME BAD NEWS...

HACK AND YO
SHALL FIN
...AND EVEN WORSE NEWS!

CAN YOUNG JUSTICE GET BACK ON THEIR FEET...?

Read the next action-packed adventure to find out!

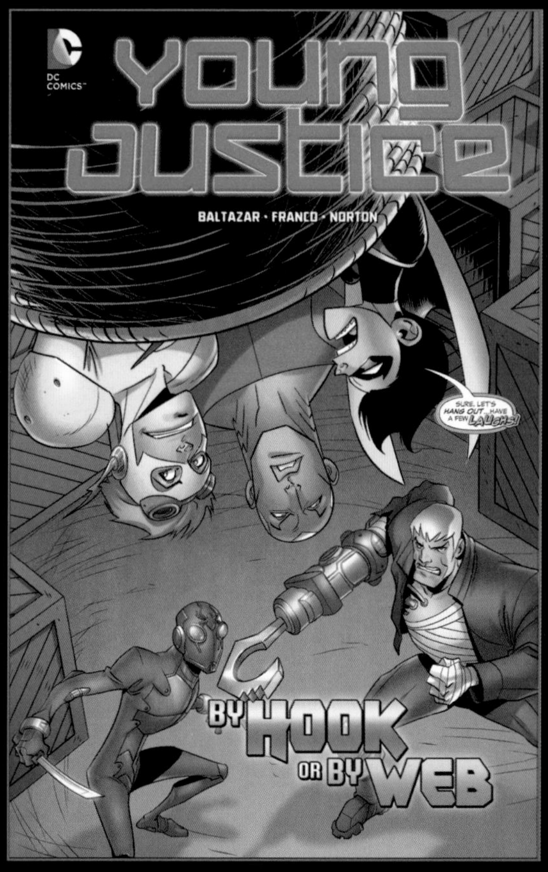

only from...

CREATORS

ART BALTAZAR WRITER

Art Baltazar is a cartoonist machine from the heart of Chicago! He defines cartoons and comics not only as an art style, but as a way of life. Currently, Art is the creative force behind *The New York Times* best-selling, Eisner Award-winning, DC Comics series Tiny Titans, and the co-writer for Billy Batson and the Magic of SHAZAM! and co-creator of Superman Family Adventures. Art is living the dream! He draws comics and never has to leave the house. He lives with his lovely wife, Rose, big boy Sonny, little boy Gordon, and little girl Audrey. Right on!

FRANCO AURELIANI WRITER

Bronx, New York born writer and artist Franco Aureliani has been drawing comics since he could hold a crayon. Currently residing in upstate New York with his wife, Ivette, and son, Nicolas, Franco spends most of his days in a Batcave-like studio where he produces DC's Tiny Titans comics. In 1995, Franco founded Blindwolf Studios, an independent art studio where he and fellow creators can create children's comics. Franco is the creator, artist, and writer of Weirdsville, L'il Creeps, and Eagle All Star, as well as the co-creator and writer of Patrick the Wolf Boy. When he's not writing and drawing, Franco also teaches high school art.

MIKE NORTON ARTIST

Mike Norton has been a professional comic book artist for more than ten years. His best-known works for DC Comics include the series Young Justice, All-New Atom, and Green Arrow/Black Canary.

GLOSSARY

allegedly (uh-LEJ-uhd-lee)--accused but not yet convicted, or presumed to be

appropriate (uh-PROH-pree-uht)--suitable or right

authorization (aw-thur-rye-ZAY-shuhn)--official permission or approval

cautious (KAW-shuhss)--if you are cautious, you try hard to avoid mistakes or danger

covert (KOH-vert)--hidden or secret

cross-referenced (KRAWSS-REF-uh-renss)--verified by multiple sources

fiasco (fee-ASS-koh)--a complete failure

hunch (HUHNCH)--an idea that is not backed by proof

maneuver (muh-NOO-ver)--a difficult movement that needs planning or skill

nauseating (NAW-zee-ay-ting)--feeling sick to your stomach

reiterate (ree-IT-uh-reyt)--to say or do again, or repeatedly

sanctioned (SANGK-shuhnd)--permitted or given approval to do something

VISUAL QUESTIONS & PROMPTS

1. Why do you think the characters are shaded and dark in this panel? What do you think it says about them? How does it make you feel? Why?

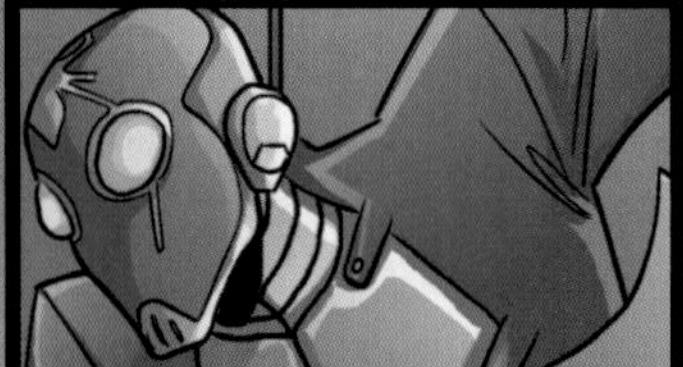

2. Identify a few ways that the two panels below show that the members of Young Justice need some more teamwork practice.

3. Based on the art in the panel to the left, what kind of movement do you think Robin did to avoid being struck? Explain.

4. Based on the surrounding panels, what do you think the Black Spider is doing when he touches his fingers to his ear in the middle panel?

5. Identify a few things that this panel tells you about what's going on in the story.

CENTRAL CITY
JULY 9, 19:54 CDT
WHY IS SHE STILL AT WORK? EVERYONE ELSE WENT HOME HOURS AGO.

YOUNG JUSTICE™

READ THEM ALL!

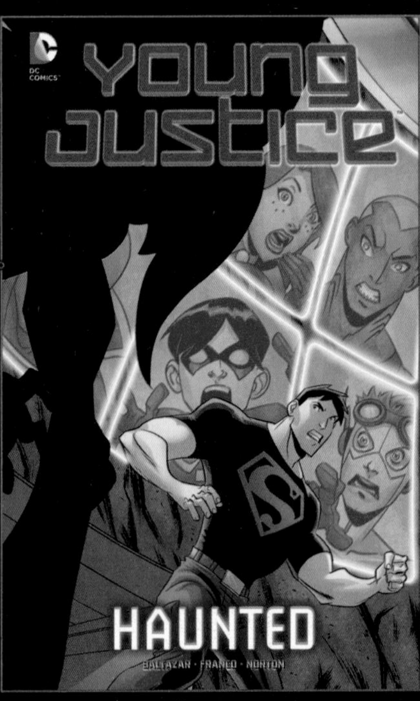

Haunted

Monkey Business

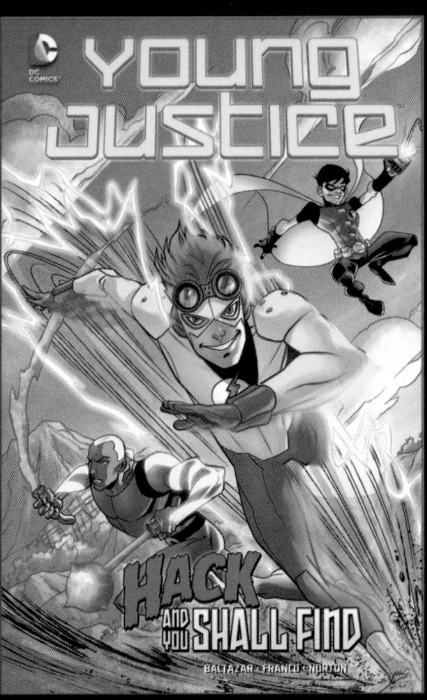

Hack and You Shall Find

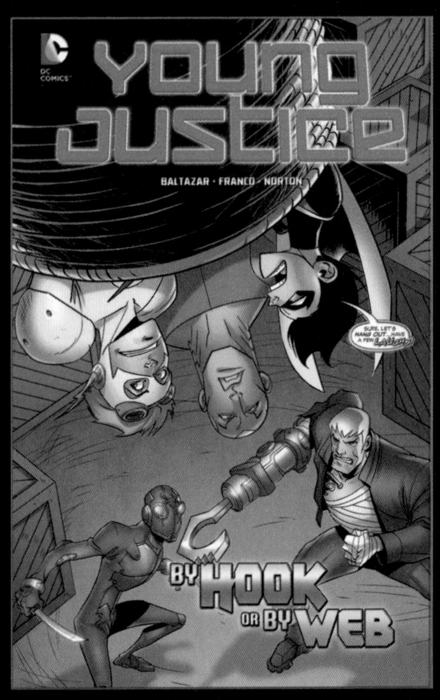

By Hook or By Web

only from...

Young Justice™